1

"Watch my lips!" Lily declared. "No more dressing up, OK?"

Amber and Pearl sighed.

Amber tried on the flowered apron which Lily had been wearing. Pearl dragged a black satin, net skirt from the dressing-up box and put it on.

"I mean it!" Lily insisted. "It's one thing listening to a fairy tale when you're a kid,

but it's different when you're actually there in Snow-White world."

"No need to tell me," Amber-Cinderella muttered. She liked Lily's Snow White apron and decided to keep it on.

"It's not fair," Pearl grumbled, twirling in her flouncy skirt. She was still upset that she hadn't been whooshed away. "I'm the only one who doesn't know what it's like."

Lily made her friend stand still. "You don't *want* to know!"

"Yes, I do!" Pearl argued. *Twirl – twirl.* Nothing!

"Listen. In Snow-White world, the wicked Queen is seriously scary. She throws people in prison and poisons you!"

"But not for real," Pearl argued.

Lily's Dressing-Up Dreams

The Pearly Comb

COMING SOON

The Pearly Comb

JENNY OLDFIELD

Hodder
Children's
Books

A division of Hachette Children's Books

First published in Great Britain in 2008
by Hodder Children's Books

1

A Catalogue record for this book is available from the British Library

ISBN-13: 978 0 340 95599 4

Printed and bound in Great Britain
by Clays Ltd St Ives plc, Bungay, Suffolk

The paper and board used in this paperback by Hodder Children's
Books are natural recyclable products made from wood grown in
sustainable forests. The manufacturing processes conform to the
environmental regulations of the country of origin.

Hodder Children's Books
A division of Hachette Children's Books
338 Euston Rd, London NW1 3BH
An Hachette Livre UK company

"Yes, for real!" Amber backed Lily up. She remembered the Uglies and the wicked stepmother in Cinderella world. Totally real.

"Puh!" Pearl sulked.

"Stop squabbling down there!" Amber's mum called from the top of the basement stairs. "Go outside and play!"

"I'm a deep-sea diver!" Amber yelled. She pretend-swam around the edge of the garden pond.

"I can see whales!" Lily cried, joining in. "There she blows!" she yelled as she faked front-crawl.

"You're nuts," Pearl grumbled. Life just wasn't fair.

"Land ahoy!" Amber shouted. Now she

was chief pirate on a pirate ship tossed by the waves. It had begun to rain. The drops plopped into the pond and splashed on her face.

"Man overboard!" Lily cried, as Pearl turned towards the house and stomped up the lawn.

"Hah, very funny!" Pearl muttered. "I'm getting wet. I'm going inside."

"OK, what shall we play now?" Amber rummaged under the cupboard in the basement.

Outside, the rain fell steadily. It dribbled down the window panes and the wind battered at the door.

"Let's play Snap!" Lily suggested

"Boring!" Amber and Pearl replied.

Pearl drifted over to the dressing-up box.

"No way!" Lily reminded her. "Never again. You can't make me!"

The rain fell all the time they were having lunch.

Then Amber had a good idea. "Let's play hairdressers!" She put a chair next to the dressing-up box. "Sit down, Lily. You can be the first customer!"

"Ouch!" Lily said as Amber picked up a brush and tugged at the tangles in her thick dark hair.

Pearl pretended to sweep hair from the floor around the chair.

"Shall I use the straighteners?" Amber asked Lily. "Would you like conditioner?"

"Pa-pom, pa-pom!" Pearl hummed as

she swept. Then she picked a silky
pink shawl from the dressing-up box to
cover Lily's chest and shoulders.
"All hairdressers give you a cape,"
she explained.

"Psst-pssst!" Amber fake-sprayed Lily's
hair. Then she held up a mirror for her to
see the effect.

"Very nice," Lily declared, looking from this side and that. Then she stood up and turned. "How much do . . . I . . . owe . . . yooooooh!"

The silk shawl began to shimmer and sparkle. A bright white light filled the basement.

"Wow, the shawl," Amber said, standing well back. "It's magic – look!"

"Rats!" Pearl said as Lily vanished.

2

"Amber and Pearl, just you wait!" Lily heard her voice drift into a big white space. She was floating again, surrounded by silvery sparkles. The pink shawl fluttered in a warm, gentle breeze.

Whoosh!

Lily was spinning as she floated. The white light grew colder until there was snow in the air – small flakes settling on her face, glittering with silver light.

"Help!" Lily cried, though she knew no one would hear. "I don't want this to happen," she protested. "I've had enough of the wicked Queen and her stupid followers. It's cold here. I want to go home!"

Queen Serena looked down at Snow White.

Lily lay in the clearing close to the cottage where the seven dwarves lived. Her eyes were closed.

"I have killed Snow White!" Queenie announced.

Two figures crept from the shadows of the tall trees. They stared at the cloaked figure on the ground.

"At last!" Her Most Royal Highness cried. The Queen had cast off the old-woman disguise and stood tall and proud in black velvet. "The child is dead from a poisoned thorn, and now I am fairest in all the land!"

"No doubt about it, Your Majesty!" Sir Manfred replied. He looked uneasily around the clearing.

"The most beautiful!" Prince Lovelace agreed. The Prince's teeth chattered and his bony knees knocked together.

Queen Serena held her head high. A cruel smile twisted her face. "Snow White will trouble us no more!" she declared. "Come, let us go back to the palace. Make haste before a blizzard traps us here in the forest!"

The quiet snow fell. Lily's eyes were closed. Flakes settled on her eyelids and eyelashes.

The snow covered their tracks. It lay on the branches of the trees and the roof of the woodshed. Wind blew white drifts against the door of the cottage.

At last the snow stopped and the air cleared.

A spotted deer trod warily into the

clearing, its bright eyes alert to danger. A second followed, then a third.

They went up to the figure lying under a layer of cold snow. Gently they poked and pushed with their noses until they uncovered Lily's pale face.

Startled, the deer stepped back. Then they moved forward again and nuzzled Lily's cheeks, but the child's eyes stayed closed.

Dead or asleep? the deer wondered.

A black crow cawed from a branch across the clearing. It flapped its wings and flew to the ground.

A red fox trotted daintily between the trees, its bushy tail whisking against the trunks.

The three deer lowered their heads.

Wake up! they said to the child. *Wake up.
Or the cold will certainly kill you!*

*

"Your Most Royal Highness, listen to me!"
Nurse Gretchen knelt before the King in
his chamber.

She'd pushed her way past guards and

footmen, determined to see the King.

"Stand aside!" Snow White's old Nurse had rolled up her sleeves and pushed strong men down like skittles. "Do not try to stop me. I must see the King!"

They'd barred her way with spears and swords, but she'd thrust the cold steel aside.

Now she was on her knees, begging him to listen. "Your Majesty, there are seven men in your dungeon. They are dwarves – brothers who work in the gold mines in the forest outside the palace gates. It is said they have stolen gold from Your Majesty."

The King looked down at Gretchen with sad eyes. The curtains in his chamber kept out the sunlight. All was dark and gloomy. "What of it?" he sighed.

"Why, they should not be there!" Gretchen declared. "They are not thieves, they are honest men!"

The King heard and roused himself from his deep sadness. "Are you certain?"

"As honest as the day. And loyal to Your Most Royal Highness!" the Nurse insisted.

She'd seen how Queen Serena had accused the seven dwarves and had thrown them in the dungeons. And Gretchen believed that they might know the secret of Snow White's disappearance.

"Why do you think this?" King Jakob asked the Nurse.

"I have lived in this palace and served Your Most Royal Highness faithfully all these years. Have I not?"

The King nodded.

19

"Then trust me, the men do not have a dishonest hair on their heads!"

"Very well, they shall be set free," King Jakob sighed. He wished to be left in peace to grieve for Snow White, but he was a fair man who wanted justice for his subjects. And he trusted the honest Nurse. "Guards!" he cried.

Two men with helmets and spears appeared at the door.

"Go to the dungeons and release the seven dwarves."

"B-b-but, Your Most Royal Highness," one stammered, "Her Most Royal Highness g-g-gave the order to put them in prison."

"Queen Serena was mistaken," the King insisted, looking stern.

The guards twitched and shuffled nervously.

But Gretchen hurried over to them, turned them around and hustled them along the corridor.

"You heard what the King said," she cried. "You must set the dwarves free!"

"Quick, before Queen Serena returns!" The second the guards unlocked the door of the dungeon, Gretchen grabbed the nearest dwarf and bundled him towards the courtyard.

"Come, brothers, we will go with the old woman!" Tom cried as he was hauled along the stone corridor and up the steps into the open air.

Jack, Roly, Pete, Will, Hans and

21

Walt shook off the prison cobwebs and followed.

"Less of the 'old'!" Gretchen grumbled. "I may be no spring chicken, but there is life in these limbs, and while I have breath in my body, I will use it to save my darling Snow White!"

*

22

Weak sunshine and crisp, frosty air greeted the dwarves.

"What about Snow White?" Tom demanded. "Tell us everything you know."

"Upon my soul!" Gretchen cried. "Men are so slow, I tell you; Snow White fled from here and the Queen followed on horseback."

"The Queen is chasing Snow White?" Will asked. This was very bad news. He felt the hairs at the back of his neck stand up and a shiver ran through him.

"Yes!" Gretchen thrust Will through the gates then rounded up the other dwarves to follow him. "Go home as fast as your legs will carry you.

"Run! Do not delay. The poor child is in grave danger!"

3

Though Roly was stout and short of breath, he led the way through the forest, forging a path for the rest.

Hans and Walt followed, running between the snow-laden trees, battling through snowdrifts, towards the cottage.

In the distance Will heard horses trampling through the frozen forest. Voices were calling.

"Stop!" Will warned the others.

The seven dwarves crouched low behind a high, smooth bank of snow.

"Make haste back to the palace," Queen Serena shouted to Sir Manfred and Prince Lovelace. "Snowflakes fly into my face. The blizzard almost blinds me."

She rode by on her black horse, her sable cloak gathered about her, the silver bridle jingling.

Two bedraggled figures trailed after her. Sir Manfred stooped over his horse's neck, fighting the wind and snow. Prince Lovelace slumped in the saddle, his frozen fingers unable to grasp the reins.

But the Queen held her head high. "Snow White is dead!" she cried out. "A poisoned thorn finished her off. Now

I am the fairest in all the land!"

At these words, Hans almost stood up in dread, but Tom held him down.

"Dead?" Walt whispered. "Are we too late? Oh brothers, my heart will break in two!"

"Hush!" Will muttered, waiting until the Queen's party had passed by. Then he sprang up and led the way. "Snow White cannot be dead!" he told himself. "Hurry, everyone. We can still save her from the wicked Queen!"

*

The three spotted deer stood beside Lily in the forest clearing. Their bodies sheltered her from the wind and their breath warmed her frozen face, until they heard footsteps. Then they faded into the forest.

"Snow White!" Will cried as he burst out from beneath the trees and saw the figure lying in the snow.

Lily tried to open her eyes. She glimpsed the world through the half-melted snowflakes on her eyelashes. All seemed blurred and dreamlike.

"Snow White, wake up!" Half a dozen voices floated around her.

Hans knelt down in the snow and took Lily's hand. "So cold," he murmured.

"But her eyelids flickered," Roly said.

"Carry her inside," Jack instructed.

Tom lifted her from the ground and carried Lily into the warmth of the cottage. He laid her down by the fire.

"Is she alive?" Walt asked, standing back a little, dreading what the answer might be.

"She lives," Pete told him, stroking the snow from Lily's cheek.

Lily's eyelids fluttered then closed again.

28

She felt the warmth of the flickering flames but she couldn't move or speak.

"What ails her?" Hans pleaded with Pete. "What can we do to help?"

Pete shook his head, then he remembered what the Queen had said as she rode by. *A poisoned thorn finished her off.* "Poison!" he said suddenly.

"That's it!" Jack cried. "The poison is still in Snow White's body. We must find a remedy – a herb or a medicine that will save her."

Then Walt came forward and took Lily gently by the hand. "There is blood on her finger," he pointed out. "And a thorn through her skin."

Quickly Jack looked at the tiny wound. "Hans, fetch some small tweezers – the ones you used to make Snow White's gold locket. We'll soon have this thorn out. Roly, boil some dried herbs in a kettle to take away the poison. Will and Tom, bring blankets."

Lily heard the dwarves rush to her aid. She felt warmer now and could see the red glow of the fire.

"Easy does it!" Jack whispered as he took the silver tweezers and carefully pulled out the thorn. Then Roly soothed the wound with the herbs and Will and Tom covered her in woollen blankets.

"Her eyes are opening again!" Hans whispered in relief.

"And she breathes more deeply," Walt murmured.

The glow grew brighter and now Lily

could see seven faces gathered round, seven pairs of eyes fixed on her, all willing her to wake up.

"Greetings, Snow White," Jack said, leaning over, patting her hand and beginning to smile. "Welcome back, my dear."

"Welcome!" Tom, Pete, Will, Hans and Walt murmured. "Take your time. How do you feel? Are you strong enough to sit?"

"Try this nice warm soup," Roly said. "It will make you strong again. Just one spoonful to line your stomach and make you well."

4

"Who set the dwarves free?" Queen Serena shrieked. She'd galloped in through the palace gates, dismounted and swept into the main hall. A quivering servant had delivered the latest news. "Where is the idiot who disobeyed my order? Find him. Throw him into the darkest dungeon and let him rot!"

"Her Most Royal Highness is back from

her ride in the forest," a footman told the King in his chamber.

"So I hear," King Jakob replied with a sigh. "Let it be known that I am tired and do not wish to be disturbed."

So he went to bed at noon with the curtains drawn to keep out the world of his wife and her angry demands.

"Set out the silver plate and deck the table with meat and wine," Queen Serena ordered. "Tonight we will have a feast."

The kitchen boys and maid-servants ran to carry out the Queen's commands, though King Jakob had ordered that there was to be no feasting for a year and a day.

"Fetch me my finest gown," Her Most Royal Highness commanded. "The crimson dress adorned with rubies, and my ruby rings and the golden crown. Invite princes from near and far. Go, girl, do as I say!"

So the servants ran hither and thither, frightened by the power-mad Queen.

"I am happy!" Serena announced to the quivering girl who dressed her hair in long braids which she coiled around her head. "I am the fairest in the land, and we will have music tonight, and dancing to celebrate."

"Aaah-tchoo!"

Outside in the corridor, someone sneezed and the maid-servant almost dropped her brush in surprise.

"Arrest that man!" Queenie yelled. "There must be no illness in the palace until after the feast."

34

"Aaah-tchoo!"

"Seize him!" the Queen screamed until guards came running and there was a scuffle outside the door.

"Your Most Royal Highness!" a high voice squealed. "Call off the guards. I have something important to say to you!"

"Prince Lovelace," Serena sighed. She thrust the hairdresser aside. "Come in, but stand as far from me as possible. If I sneeze and my nose turns red before the feast tonight, I will have you thrown . . ."

". . . In the dungeon." The poor Prince knew what punishment awaited him if he passed on his germs. He came in and stood shivering by the door.

The Queen stood and faced him. "Well, get on with it." Queenie took up a lace hankie and held it over her nose and mouth. "I have only five short hours to get ready for the feast. Tell me your important news and then be gone."

Prince Lovelace spoke through his blocked nose. "I have in my possession something that will interest you . . ."

"Oh, for goodness sake!" Queenie snapped. "Show me and go!"

The shaking Prince pulled an item from the pocket of his yellow brocade jacket and held it flat in the palm of his hand.

"A gold locket?" Queen Serena frowned. "Of what interest is that bauble to me?"

"This is not any old locket," the Prince explained. "Aah-tchoo! This is the locket I snatched from Snow White's neck when she made her escape."

"Show me!" Queenie ran to grab the locket. Sure enough, it bore Snow White's initials. "But what use is this locket to me now?"

"Give it to the King," Lovelace replied. "Tell him it was found by Snow White's body. It is more proof that she is dead."

"Hmm." Serena turned the locket in her palm. "The King is already drowning in sorrow at the loss of Snow White," she reminded herself. "This locket will break his poor heart in two."

"Exactly!" Lovelace said nervously. "Then the King would be dead and you would rule the land!"

"Wicked!" the Queen murmured, her eyes lighting up at the thought. "Prince Lovelace, that is a black and treacherous thought."

Lovelace quivered and trembled all over, expecting the worst.

But the Queen's face broke into an evil smile. "You are a man after my own cruel heart!" she declared. "And, Prince Lovelace, if you didn't have a cold, I would clasp you in my royal embrace!"

The Prince beamed and bowed. "Aaah . . ."

". . . Tchoo!" Queenie slammed the door in his face mid-sneeze. "Thank you!" she hissed, folding her long fingers over the locket. "I will show this pathetic bauble to the King on my way to the feast tonight!"

5

Queen Serena was dressed in her crimson gown. Rubies sparkled on her fingers. A golden crown glinted on her head.

In the great hall, trumpeters announced the arrival of the Prince of Ice Mountain and the handsome Duke of the Night Forest.

The Queen gazed in her mirror. She smoothed her gown with her tapered fingers then went to a small carved table and picked up Snow White's locket.

"I will break the King's heart!" she said quietly. "Then I will feast with the Prince and the Duke."

But before she left her chamber, she stole one last look in her magic mirror. And vanity overcame her.

"Tell me, glass," she whispered, a satisfied smile playing around the corners of her mouth. "Tell me true! Of all the ladies of the land, Who is the fairest? Tell me who?"

The Queen gazed at herself in the mirror and waited for it to reply – "Thou, Queen, art fairest in the land."

She waited a long time. Her reflection seemed to shake and blur, as if water had been poured over the smooth surface. Then it cleared again.

"Tell me, glass, tell me true!" the Queen urged. "Of all the ladies in the land, Who is the fairest? Tell me who?"

The mirror replied at last. "Thou, Queen, mayst fair and beauteous be, But Snow White is lovelier far than thee!"

At this Serena gasped and turned deathly pale. She flew into a rage, taking the glass from its hook and throwing it down. Then she tore pictures from the wall and smashed them, ripped her fine silk sheets and dashed her box of jewels against the wall. Sapphires and diamonds, emeralds and precious pearls scattered across the floor.

"Alive!" the Queen hissed, her body

shaking with rage. She flung Lily's locket through the window. "I left Snow White for dead and now I find she lives!"

Anger swept over her in waves. "I will seek her out," she swore, striding to her window. She stared up at the star-studded heavens. "I will leave no stone unturned until I find her and destroy her once and for all!"

"The Queen will stop at nothing," Pete warned his brothers while Snow White slept.

Jack nodded. "I'm afraid you're right."

"But we will take care of Snow White and keep her safe." Hans felt it was his turn to speak out. "There are seven of us and only one of the wicked Queen."

"But the Queen is powerful," Will reminded his kindly, clumsy brother. "And people are afraid of her. They will do her bidding."

Again Jack agreed. He turned to Pete, who sat deep in thought. "What shall we do, brother? How can we keep the child out of the Queen's clutches?"

Pete rubbed his temples. He sighed then bit his lip. At last he came up with his best solution. "We must leave the cottage and take Snow White deeper into the forest, where no one may find us."

"Leave the cottage!" Roly echoed. "How will we live? What will we eat?"

"We will take food with us," Pete explained. "Enough to last us through the winter. We will seek shelter, perhaps at the entrance to one of the mines, close to the foot of Ice Mountain."

"But there are wolves out there in the wild," Will reminded him. "And no paths through the forest."

"Which is exactly why we must go there," Jack decided for them all. "Pete is right as usual. We must choose a hiding place where no one will follow. Only then will Snow White be safe."

So the dwarves packed up and set off at dusk, when Snow White was refreshed and the thorn was only a bad memory.

"Wear your thick cloak. Line your boots with heavy socks. Pull your hood around your face." Tom fussed over Lily as they locked the door of the cottage and began their trek through the forest.

"I'm OK," she assured him. "Sad to leave, but I'm feeling fine – thanks."

"No wobbles?" Roly checked. "Did the hot soup do the job?"

Lily smiled and nodded. "And the nice long sleep. But where exactly are we going?" she asked, peering ahead under the trees.

"Where the Queen will not find us," Walt promised, remembering word for word what Jack had said. "We are going where no one will follow."

"With our lanterns and our pickaxes," Pete pointed out. "By day we will work in the gold mines. We will return to the shelter each night, the same as before."

But it won't be the same, Lily thought, glancing over her shoulder at the dark cottage. She would miss its cosy warmth, its row of seven beds covered with seven quilts and the seven plates set out on the long table for supper each night. *No, not the same at all!*

OK, now I'm really scared. I don't like this place one little bit!

Lily didn't grumble out loud. After all,

Jack and the gang had done their best with the entrance to the mine shaft. They'd cleared out some of the cobwebs and chased the spiders away. They'd hung lanterns and stopped the icy draught at the entrance.

It's like living in a cave. Lily stayed awake as the brothers slept. She stared up at the rough stone roof. *It's smelly and damp.*

Then Lily heard Amber's voice telling her not to be such a wuss. *So what if it's damp? This is all the dwarves could find. You have to toughen up and get on with it!*

The toughen-up voice was so real that Lily sat up and checked the dark shelter. No, there was no one here.

Then Lily remembered how she and the seven dwarves had walked in the dark for hours, using their knowledge of the forest, trudging from one mine to the next until they'd reached this one – a shaft which had lain unused for many years. The track leading to it was overgrown with brambles and blocked by fallen trees. The door at the entrance creaked on its hinges and the only inhabitants were bats and mice.

Bats! Lily thought she spied some hanging from the roof and shivered. *At*

this rate I'm never going to get a wink of sleep!

But in the morning Lily felt much more cheerful.

Walt made a fire out of dry sticks. Roly lit it and soon there was a pan of porridge steaming away.

OK, it's like camping, Lily decided.

Hans came in with fresh water from a nearby stream. "I didn't spill a drop!" he announced.

Like being in the Brownies, only for real! Lily thought.

So she got busy – scouting around for brushwood that would make a broom to sweep the floor while the dwarves were out at work, making a duster out of feathers gathered outside the door.

"Always sweeping and tidying!" Will laughed as he put on his boots ready to go to work.

"Pa-pom-pom-pom!" Lily hummed. She swept the dirt from their shelter and put a cloth over the makeshift table which Roly had made from old planks of wood. "Pom-pom-pa-pom!" She dusted cobwebs from the walls then set candles on ledges to brighten the gloom.

Soon the brothers were ready to leave

for a day's work at the mine.

"Do not set foot out of the shelter," Tom warned Lily as he picked up his pickaxe.

"Stay inside and keep warm," Pete insisted. "Remember, you must not talk to anyone."

"I promise!" Lily replied happily. She had brought needles and thread with her, and a heap of unmended shirts and socks. There was plenty to do.

So the dwarves set off through the snow, singing as they went.

"Pa-pom!" Lily hummed as she put away the broom. "Doo-do-di-doodle-doo!"

The day went on and the silence of the frozen forest surrounded her.

"It's beautiful!" Lily murmured, staring

out through the door at the snow crystals glistening on the smooth drifts. Long icicles formed on the branches bent low under the weight of the snow.

Silent and still, the day passed.

So quiet! Lily said to herself, looking out at the sun's rays which filtered between the branches. The silence seemed to wrap itself around her like the silver threads of a butterfly's cocoon. *Queenie is in the palace far away. She can throw hissy fits and send out search parties. But she'll never, never find me!*

6

That morning King Jakob set out from the palace on his white horse. He went alone, slipping away when no one was looking, wanting only silence for his sorrowful thoughts. He rode far into the forest.

I am a rich man, he thought as he passed the dwarves' empty cottage. *But the poorest man in the kingdom is happier than me, for he has not lost a daughter as I have, and he does not know the grief I feel.*

The sad King rode on. Soon there were no paths between the trees and the snow was untrodden. Ahead lay the mighty peak of Ice Mountain.

"I would give away my whole kingdom," he said to the deer hiding in the snowy thicket, "if only I could have Snow White back."

The startled deer ran away. A speckled hawk rose from a branch and flew off.

"We would live in a cottage. There would be no crowns and fine gowns, only sunlight and happiness in our lives."

On the King rode, his strong white horse carrying him. They went past mine shafts and heard the hammering of the miners way below ground.

Then, further still, through endless, untracked forest.

"Three – four – five – six!" Lily made a pile of the pairs of socks she had mended. Then she stood up and stretched. She peered out of the door of the shelter.

"Blue sky!" she said, gazing up through the heavy branches.

Crunch-crunch. A horse's footsteps approached and Lily darted back inside.

Crunch. The horse plodded nearer. Lily realised that she'd left the door ajar.

"I would give the whole world for one glimpse of Snow White!" King Jakob sighed as he rode by.

Lily flew to the door and pushed it shut. She hardly dared to breathe as the horse passed by. *The King!* she thought. *Poor man, his heart's breaking!*

She could ease his sorrow. She could open the door and run from the shelter. He would throw his arms around her and his wish would come true. But . . .!

"Snow White, with her hair black as a raven's wing and skin white as snow," King Jakob murmured softly.

. . . But then there was Queenie!

If Lily dashed out now and went home with the King, Her Most Royal Highness would be there, green with envy, talking to her mirror and swearing to kill Snow White all over again.

As Lily hesitated, more horses approached and men in cloaks and wide-brimmed hats surrounded the King.

"Your Most Royal Highness," one rider began, sweeping off his hat and bowing low over his horse's neck.

Lily peeped through a crack in the door and saw that the messenger was none other than Sir Manfred.

"Her Most Royal Highness, Queen Serena has sent us to bring you back to the palace. She is afraid you will come to harm, out here in the forest."

King Jakob frowned at the lords on horseback. "I am King of this land," he said sternly. "I may ride where I wish."

"By all means, Your Majesty," another of the riders agreed.

Prince Pester-Face! Lily gritted her teeth and tried not to move. If she gave herself away now, she was in deep trouble. And the dwarves too. *Don't move a muscle!*

"But Your Royal Highness might catch your death of cold," the Prince went on. "The Queen is afraid for your safety . . ."

"Yes, yes," King Jakob sighed wearily. He realised his solitary ride was at an end. "I will ride no further."

He reined his horse back in the direction he had come.

Sir Manfred, Prince Lovelace and the

rest nodded and grasped each other by the gloved hand. They had found the King and were bringing him home. The Queen would be pleased with them and they would escape her wrath.

Inside the shelter, Lily waited until the last footfall had died away. Then she dared to peer out at the patch of trampled snow.

"That was close!" she sighed, seeing by the fall of the shadows on the ground that the sun had passed its peak and they were halfway through the long afternoon.

"What now?" Lily wandered aimlessly round the small shelter.

Crunch, crunch. More horse's footsteps approached. They were unsteady and this rider's voice was high and panicky.

Lily went back to the door and peered out through the crack.

"Oh my, oh dear!" the rider cried. "Ooh my old bones are creaking, I am frozen from top to toe!"

Nurse Gretchen! Lily couldn't believe her ears. She opened the door to see.

Creak! The old door was rusty on its hinges. *Creak-creak!*

The Nurse's horse heard the sudden sound and reared up.

"Help!" Gretchen cried. She fell back in the saddle then tossed forward as her horse bucked. He threw the poor old Nurse to and fro like a rocking-horse.

"Ouch!" Lily half closed her eyes.

"Oh!" Gretchen cried, looking like a bag of old laundry in the saddle. Her brown skirt billowed, her shawl flapped. "Oof!"

"Ouch!" Lily said again as she heard a loud thud.

Gretchen had been thrown from her horse. She landed in a snowdrift and the mount galloped off.

"Help!" the Nurse cried as she floundered in the snow. "Come back, you silly old bag of bones. Come back!"

But there was silence as the horse ran to catch up with the King and his lords.

What do I do now? Lily wondered. Tom and Pete's words rang inside her head. "Do not set foot outside this shelter . . .

Talk to no one!"

Outside, Gretchen struggled to stand up in the deep drift. She stumbled away then tripped over a hidden tree root. Down she went again, waist deep in snow.

But this is Gretchen! Lily told herself. *She's on my side!*

"I'm done for!" the Nurse cried as she settled into the freezing drift. "Oh, how my bones ache. And to think, I shall never see my dove, my darling, ever again!"

That's me! Lily thought. *I'm her dove, her darling!*

It was too much to bear – she opened the door and dashed outside.

"Ohhh!" Nurse Gretchen gasped. She saw Lily standing at the entrance to the shelter. "Are you a dream?"

"No, I'm real!" Lily cried, dashing forward to haul the Nurse out of the drift. But she missed her footing and she too fell waist deep.

"My duckling, my lovely girl, I risked my life on that old nag to follow the lords and search for you!" Gretchen sighed, clasping Lily in her stout arms. Then she drew out a gold locket with a broken chain and handed it to Lily. "I found it lying on the ground in the palace courtyard," she explained. "I saw the initials and knew it was yours, my dove."

"Thank you!" Lily cried, delighted.

But as the Nurse gave Lily the locket, they overbalanced and fell backwards down a slope, floundering and struggling, skidding and sliding.

"Ouch!" Lily cried as they hit a root.

"Oof!" Nurse Gretchen held on to Lily as she hit a sturdy tree trunk which brought them to a sudden stop.

Still the Nurse embraced Lily. She hugged her until the breath was almost squeezed out of her.

Then she let her go and gently wiped the snow from Lily's face. There were tears running down her broad, wrinkled face. "My own girl, I have found you at last!"

65

7

"Whoa!" Lily had to stop Gretchen from squeezing the living daylights out of her. She broke free and set off up the slope.

The Nurse clambered up the bank after her. "The Queen is mad with jealousy," she gasped as she struggled up the hill. "She flings people in the dungeons who only glance at her or cross her path by chance. The cells are full to overflowing."

"That's not right." Lily shook snow from her skirt and invited the Nurse into the shelter.

"And every hour the Queen sends out a fresh search party to find you, my dove."

"OK, so she's looked in the mirror and found I'm still not dead," Lily concluded.

Gretchen sighed and nodded, warming her feet by the fire.

Lily fetched a blanket and wrapped it around Gretchen's legs. "So sooner or later, do you think, the Queen's men will discover this place?"

Gretchen nodded. "Sooner rather than later, if a silly old fool such as I can do it. Believe me, my dove, nowhere is safe."

"And this is what you wanted to tell

me?" Lily was grateful to the faithful old Nurse. "To keep me up to date with what's happening at the palace?"

"Yes. And besides, I could not stay to hear that wicked woman hatch plots against you. I had rather starve and beg than serve her a moment longer."

"Thank you for being so brave," Lily said quietly. Gretchen's news had upset her, though she tried to stay cheerful. "And no more talk about begging. You can stay here as long as you like and help me mend the dwarves' socks!"

"Ah, my sparrow, it does my heart good to see you smile," Gretchen declared. Then she stirred herself and set about snipping the wicks of the candles on the ledges, trying to make herself useful. "We need more wood for the fire," she decided, putting her shoes back on and pulling her shawl around her shoulders.

"Jack and the others will fetch it when they get back from the mine," Lily told her, but Gretchen was set in her ways.

"When I see a thing that needs doing, I do it," she declared, opening the door and letting in a strong gust of wind. "My dear Snow White, you have known me long enough to know that!"

And she set off into the forest, brushing aside the snow and picking up firewood from under the trees.

Lily watched Gretchen take off her shawl and gather the wood into it. She saw that the blue sky had clouded over and left behind a dim grey light. Then she heard a sudden yell.

"Aaagh!" Gretchen cried, throwing up her arms and scattering her firewood. She grasped at a nearby tree branch, but it was weak and snapped as she fell – tumbling down and down into darkness.

Lily felt her stomach churn as the Nurse suddenly vanished. Without thinking, she ran from the shelter and peered down the hole in the ground. Then she called Gretchen's name and waited.

There was no reply. Instead, Lily heard the dreaded sound of riders galloping.

"Nurse!" Lily cried. "Can you hear me?"

"Ye-e-s!" came the faltering voice from way below.

"Phew!" Lily looked round swiftly. Every shadow seemed to move. "You fell down a mine shaft! The entrance must have been hidden by the snow. Are you OK?"

"I've been tossed about like a cork on the ocean!" Nurse Gretchen moaned. "But no bones are broken and now I'm wedged securely on a stout plank."

"I can't see a thing!" Lily sighed, lying flat and peering into blackness. "I've no idea how I'm going to get you out and I hear horsemen galloping towards us."

"Run to the shelter," Gretchen told her. "Shut the door and hide yourself. Leave this to me!"

So Lily fled to safety and took up position, peering through the crack in the old door.

"Aaagh!" Gretchen bellowed as three riders appeared. They were dressed in black cloaks and fur hats. Swords hung at their sides. "Aaaaghhh!" she yelled at the top of her voice.

The riders reined back their horses and leaped from their saddles. They ran to track down the source of the yells.

"Aha!" One man knelt by the opening to the old shaft. "Ho, who's down there? Are you hurt?"

"Help!" Gretchen groaned. "Oh, I have broken every limb in my poor body. I shall die if you do not help!"

But she told me she wasn't badly hurt, Lily thought. *What's going on? Oh, I get it. She's making a big thing of it to keep the men away from the shelter!*

"Ohhhhh!" Gretchen groaned.

"Keep still, don't move," the man yelled.

"Uh-uhhh!"

"Bring a rope!" he ordered the second rider. "It seems an old woman has got stuck down this shaft."

"Let's leave her to die," the third man suggested. "The Queen will be angry if we leave off our search for Snow White."

"Aaaaaaghhhh!" Gretchen put in an extra-loud groan. "I am Snow White's old Nurse. I have important news for Her Most Royal Highness!"

Huh? Lily strained to hear the Nurse's faint command. *Did I hear that right? Is Nurse Gretchen going to rat on me?*

The three searchers heard loud and clear. "What news?" the first man yelled down the shaft.

"It's a secret!" Gretchen insisted. "I can

only tell the Queen!"

Yes, she is – no, she wouldn't, she couldn't possibly . . . Lily dithered. What if the Nurse was truly planning to betray her?

Or was this a clever decoy?

The first man slung the rope down the shaft. He told Gretchen to grab it and not let go. "Nurse, have you seen Snow White somewhere in the forest?" he demanded.

"My news is for the Queen's ears only," Gretchen insisted, huffing and puffing as she was raised to the surface.

Lily listened hard. She heard the men heave and grunt. Risking another peep, she saw Gretchen's head appear and then her stout body and legs.

"Oh me, oh my!" Gretchen groaned, pulling her skirt straight then sinking

against the nearest rescuer. "You must take me back to the palace!"

"But we have been sent to search for Snow White." The harsh rider spoke up. "The Queen says we must not return without her."

From behind the shelter door, Lily swallowed hard. Could Gretchen keep up the act and lead the men away?

"The palace!" Gretchen groaned, lolling back against her rescuer. "The Queen . . .

Snow White . . . I have news!"

"Quickly, before she faints, lift her on to my horse," the first rescuer decided.

The second man agreed.

Only the third gazed sourly through the trees, perhaps spotting the door to Lily's shelter and taking a step or two towards it.

Oh no! Lily ran to blow out the candles and push the table against the door in case he tried to get in. But it was too heavy and she couldn't shift it.

"Ludwig, come and help us get the old woman into the saddle!" the first man yelled. "She is a dead weight. Come back, man. We must ride for the palace as if our lives depended on it!"

"Ohhhhh!" the Nurse groaned as the men slung her across the saddle. "The

76

Queen . . . Snow White . . . Make haste!"

Lily heard scuffles as the three men remounted their horses. She heard the bridles jingle as they turned towards the palace.

And they left Lily alone in the shelter, still clutching her gold locket, fearing for the brave Nurse and dreading every sound, every shadow in the vast, silent forest.

8

"What's for supper?" Hans asked Roly as the dwarves filed in through the door of the shelter and put down their pickaxes.

"What would you like?" Roly chuckled. "We have sausages, sausages or . . . sausages!"

"Then I'll have . . ."

"Sausages!" the five other dwarves chorused heartily.

Lily found the frying pan and handed it to Roly. Soon supper was sizzling and the brothers began to relax after their hard day down the mine.

"So, Snow White, how did you keep yourself busy?" Jack asked, sitting down at the table. "Tell us about your day."

"I swept and dusted," she answered slowly. "Then I mended socks."

Pete listened in. He put his head to one side and stared thoughtfully at Lily. "And?" he prompted after a short silence.

"That's it," she shrugged, sitting next to Jack. She was afraid that if she came straight out with the other stuff about King Jakob and Nurse Gretchen, it would send the dwarves into a panic.

"Thank you for my socks," Hans said,

shyly reclaiming two pairs from the pile of mending before joining the rest for supper.

Roly dished out the sausages with a heap of mashed potato and gravy.

"So no one passed by?" Pete asked Lily. "You didn't talk to anyone?"

"Ah." She frowned. Trust Pete to force an answer from her. "Actually, yes."

Straight away the seven brothers put down their knives and forks and stared at

Lily. "Who? When? Why didn't you say?"

"I didn't want to worry you," Lily mumbled. "First off, the King came out riding alone. He passed this way, but I stayed inside and kept well hidden until his lords came and took him back to the palace."

"Good girl!" Will said. "Well done." He dug into his pile of mash.

"Then?" Pete asked.

"Then Nurse Gretchen came looking for me." Lily faltered and bit her lip. "I went out to meet her."

"Oh dear." Sensible Tom sounded disappointed. "Maybe that wasn't such a good idea."

"But Gretchen *loves* me!" Lily protested. "She wouldn't betray me."

"And then what happened?" Jack asked.

"She says the Queen is sending lots of men into the forest because she found out from the mirror I'm still alive, and . . ."

"Stop!" Jack held up his hand. He saw immediately what this might mean. "Where is the Nurse now, my dear? Tell us quickly."

So Lily told them that the searchers had rescued Gretchen and carted her off to the palace.

"Stop!" Jack said again. He turned to his six brothers. "This is dangerous."

"Very," Pete agreed.

"Even if the Nurse is loyal to Snow White," Will added. "The Queen knows how to force facts out of people."

Roly, Tom, Hans and Walt nodded hastily. "What do we do now?" Tom asked.

"Think very hard," Pete replied.

So the food went cold on the plates until Walt, always the slowest of them all to speak, came up with his idea. "We have tried our best to help Snow White," he pointed out. "And we love her with all our hearts. But we're only poor, common men," he went on. "The Queen is rich and powerful."

"So?"

"So Snow White needs someone strong to help her," Walt explained. Then he faltered. "But who is stronger than our Queen?" he asked, shaking his head.

For a while the dwarves seemed

to be rather uncertain.

"I like the way you think, Walt," Jack said kindly. "But I'm afraid I have no answer to your last question."

"Me neither," Tom and Pete said sadly.

"Not the King, that's for sure," Will sighed. "The King is too burdened with grief to show his strength."

There was a long silence then out of the blue Walt spoke again. "Another Queen would be as strong as our Queen, isn't that true?"

There was another moment's silence then Pete thumped his fist on the table. "You're right, Walt! Another Queen! Think, brothers – who lives over yonder, behind Ice Mountain?"

"Aha!" Jack's face lit up. He stood and

went to slap Walt on the back. "The Queen of Ice Mountain. She is by all accounts a kind and generous lady."

Lily nodded eagerly. "Yes she is – I've met her."

"Is she as they say?" Tom asked.

"Very nice," Lily replied. "She came to a party at the palace after the King had been out hunting. She told me I was pretty."

"Good, good," Will said eagerly.

"Gretchen likes her too. When it got too dangerous for me to stay at the palace, Gretchen sent me off to try and reach her. She said the Queen of Ice Mountain would help me, but I never got further than your cottage."

"All this is very good," Jack decided.

"And I like Walt's idea that we need strength to fight strength. Indeed, I think we should set off at dawn tomorrow to climb the mountain and reach the land beyond."

"Agreed!" Tom, Roly, Pete, Will and Hans spoke as one.

"Agreed, Walt?" Jack asked.

Slowly Walt nodded. "*Before* dawn," he insisted. "We will set off to climb the mountain. Snow White, you will stay here and wait for us to return. We will bring help from the good Queen. All will be well.

What I really want more than anything is a lovely hot bath! Lily imagined what she would do when the Queen of Ice

Mountain came to her rescue.

Jack, Tom, Roly, Pete, Will, Hans and Walt had set off as planned after only a few hours of restless sleep. Lily had stayed behind, locked the door of the shelter and daydreamed.

A hot bath with lots of bubbles. Nice, smelly soap and a big soft sponge . . .!

"What a wuss!" Lily imagined how Amber and Pearl would scoff. "You're such a softie, Lily. What harm did a little bit of dirt ever do?"

Lily shrugged to herself. *Big white towels, shampoo and conditioner, those little scented candles . . .*

"Dream on!" Pearl's imaginary voice broke in again. "This is the olden days. They haven't invented shampoo, and no way do they have conditioner!"

"Whatever!" Lily sighed. "All I know is, I'm tired of roughing it. The Brownies can keep their sleeping-bags and boiling kettles over campfires. Give me a lovely warm duvet any day!"

She grew restless and began to wander around the room. Through the crack in the door she saw that the sun was already high in the sky, which meant that by now the dwarves might have made it to the top of Ice Mountain.

Soon they would come back with soldiers and maybe even the Queen of Ice Mountain herself . . .

At midday Lily snoozed in a chair. At one o'clock she made herself a sandwich. At two, she opened the door a tiny crack to let in the light.

She peered outside and saw a small brown wren take flight from a nearby log. "Nice and sunny," she murmured, venturing a step outside the door.

To her surprise, there was a woman on a white horse riding through the forest. She was a fair way off, but Lily could hear the silver bridle jingling in the clear, still air.

"Wow!" she gasped, her eyes wide, her

heart skipping a beat. "The dwarves made it to Ice Mountain in double-quick time!"

And Lily ran forward to greet the kind Queen.

Lily ran through the snow, between the tall trees. Her heart pounded with delight.

Little fool! Queen Serena said to herself, seeing Snow White rush to greet her. *Why is she running from her hiding place and showing herself to me? Surely I am the last person she wants to see.*

The wicked Queen pulled her black veil in front of her face and kept her fur collar high around her pale face. Then she turned and signalled to Sir Manfred and Prince Lovelace to keep out of sight.

Now Lily spotted the Queen on her white horse – just like the one she'd ridden from Ice Mountain when she came to King Jakob's feast.

"Your Majesty!" she cried, reaching the Queen and dropping a low curtsey.

"Thank you for coming to rescue me!"

Rescue? Her Most Royal Highness stared down at Lily from behind her thick veil.

Lily was too excited to notice that the Queen didn't speak. She jumped up and let all her fears melt away in a rush of words. "The dwarves must have found an easy way around Ice Mountain to bring you here so fast. It's so kind of you to set out yourself to find me. Where are your lords and servants? Are they bringing an extra horse for me to ride back on?"

Aha! Queen Serena saw what had happened. She smiled wickedly behind her veil. *I must alter my voice. I must play the good Samaritan!*

"Where are Jack and the rest?" Lily asked, glancing up at Ice Mountain as if expecting to spot the dwarves coming on foot down the icy slope.

"They are tired," the Queen replied in a false voice. "They are safe inside my palace, waiting for you."

"Oh good!" Lily's brown eyes sparkled. She had her sights on that nice warm bubble bath. Tonight, she and the brothers would sit at a long polished table with beautiful silver plates. Roly wouldn't have to cook. They wouldn't have a worry in the world.

"And you too must be tired, Snow White," the Queen went on. Gracefully she dismounted from her fine white horse. "My poor child, you look weary."

"Yes, I'm sorry I look such a mess," Lily said, suddenly conscious of the stains on her apron and tangles in her hair. She blushed and shook the snow from the hem of her long skirt.

"Her Most Royal Highness, Queen Serena has treated you cruelly," the Queen said, her voice high and light, though her veiled eyes were black with spite.

"You wouldn't believe how wicked she's been!" Lily declared. "Every time she finds out from her mirror that I'm still alive, she sets out to try and kill me!"

"How she has made you suffer!" the Queen sighed. She took Lily by the hand. "But now we must clean you up and make you tidy before I take you with me to my palace."

Eagerly Lily nodded. She pointed back

towards the shelter. "I've got a hairbrush in there somewhere. Just give me five minutes . . ."

"No, no, no." The Queen refused to let go of Lily's hand. "Wait. I have a beautiful pearl comb in the pocket of my cloak. Yes, here it is!"

And she drew from the velvet folds a comb made of tortoiseshell set with dozens of tiny, glowing pearls. She handed it to Lily.

"That's lovely!" Lily said, turning the precious comb and finding that the underside was as pretty as the top. She felt awkward about accepting it. "But it's too good for me to use."

"No," the Queen insisted, her grip tightening a little. "I'm offering it to you,

Snow White. It is a small gift, the first of many."

Lily looked up at the Queen's veiled features and smiled. "Thank you," she said politely, as you would to an aunt who'd given you a Christmas present you didn't really want.

"Use it," the Queen instructed, her eyes glittering, her voice gaining a hard edge as she grew more impatient. "It is a special comb, my dear. It will take away those tangles in an instant."

So reluctantly Lily put the pearl comb to her thick hair and ran the fine teeth through it.

Queen Serena reached out and quickly put her gloved hand over Lily's small fingers. She pressed the comb hard against her head.

"Ouch!" Lily cried as the comb pricked her scalp.

Then the Queen stood back and lifted her veil. "Little fool!" she said in her own voice, a cruel smile upon her lips.

And Lily gasped at the mistake she had made. "Serena!"

The Queen laughed. "Vanity has been

your undoing, Snow White, for if you had not wanted to make yourself beautiful, you would not have used the comb!"

"That's not right," Lily protested as her head began to swim and she grew dizzy. "I only did it to please you!"

Queen Serena's smile did not weaken. "The comb is poisoned and its teeth are sharp!" she announced. "I made sure it pricked through the skin. How do you feel now, Snow White? Does the world grow blurred? Do you feel faint?"

"I . . . I . . ." Lily murmured. The snow was too white. It glittered like a million diamonds.

"Yes, much too late!" the Queen scoffed as Lily swooned. "You walked into my trap, Snow White. And this time you will not escape!"

10

"You will not escape . . .!" Lily heard the wicked Queen's voice trail after her as she drifted into a white world of sparkling snow and brittle, tinkling icicles.

"Help!" she cried feebly.

She was drifting, floating, losing touch with Snow-White world.

The last thing Lily saw was the wicked Queen standing in the forest, her black

101

veil lifted to reveal her
glittering eyes and
cruel red mouth. "At
last I am the fairest in
the land!" she called
in triumph.

Lily was swept
away in a swirl of
snowflakes which sparkled like diamonds.

Cool! she thought. *This is like real flying!*

She looked down and saw the tops of the
trees, felt herself swept higher, over Ice
Mountain, way up into the blue sky.

Then there was no land below – only
white mist. She seemed to twirl gently in
the air, round and round as if her body
weighed no more than a feather and the

breeze could push her this way and that.

Now it's like floating in the sea, she thought. *It feels so-o-o good!*

*

"Why did you have to give Lily the pink shawl in the first place?" Amber asked Pearl. They stood face to face in Amber's cellar. "It was your fault that Lily got whooshed away again!"

"How was I to know the shawl was magic?" Pearl tossed her curly hair back from her freckled face.

"And now she's back in Snow-White world, and we've no idea how long she's going to be!" Amber was worried. She looked at her watch and said, "It's almost time for Lily's dad to come and pick her up. He's supposed to be taking her to Brownies."

"So-o-o good!" Lily sighed as she floated in a white and silver cloud.

Pearl and Amber turned to see a chink of bright light escaping from the dressing-up box. They ran to it and threw open the lid. A brilliant white light filled the room.

Lily opened her eyes. She threw aside a pair of fairy wings, a bent wand and a tinsel tiara then she clambered out of Amber's dressing-up box.

Pearl ran and grabbed Lily by the hand. "Tell Amber it wasn't my fault!" she insisted. "Tell her I was the one who wanted to get whooshed off, remember!"

"Whoa!" Lily stood unsteadily in

Amber's basement. She put her hand to her head and felt for the comb lodged there. "All I remember is Amber doing my hair."

"Let me do it," Pearl tutted, finding the pearl comb and pulling it free. "Hey, where did you get this?"

But just then there was a knock at the back door and the girls heard Lily's dad's voice.

"Sorry, I've got to go!" Lily said hurriedly.

"B-b-but!" Pearl and Amber protested.

"No time to explain. I'm off to Brownies. I'm doing my Tidiness badge!"

And Lily tore off her flowered apron and threw it into the box. She dashed up the steps and slammed the door after her.

"So?" Pearl said, showing Amber

the precious pearls set into the brown tortoiseshell.

"So . . ." Amber echoed softly. "Are the pearls real, or what?"

Pearl turned the comb over then shrugged. "Who knows?" She heard Lily's dad's car start and drive away. "I guess we're just going to have to wait until next time to find out."

107

Have you checked out...

www.dressingupdreams.net

It's the place to go for games, downloads, activities, sneak previews and lots of fun!

You'll find a special dressing-up game and lots of activities and fun things to do, as well as news on Dressing-Up Dreams and all your favourite characters.

Sign up to the newsletter at **www.dressingupdreams.net** to receive extra clothes for your Dressing-Up Dreams doll and the opportunity to enter special members only competitions.

What happens next...?

Log on to www.dressingupdreams.net for a sneak preview of my next adventure!

WIN A *Dressing-Up Dreams* GOODIE BAG!

CAN YOU SPOT THE TWO DIFFERENCES AND THE HIDDEN LETTER IN THESE TWO PICTURES OF THE EVIL QUEEN?

There is a spot-the-difference picture and hidden letter in the back of all four Dressing-Up Dreams books about Lily (look for the books with 5, 6, 7 or 8 on the spine). Hidden in one of the pictures above is a secret letter. Find all four letters and put them together to make a special Dressing-Up Dreams word, then send it to us. Each month, we will put the correct entries in a draw and one lucky winner will receive a magical Dressing-Up Dreams goodie bag including an exclusive Dressing-Up Dreams keyring!

Send your magical word, your name and your address
on a postcard to: **Lily's Dressing-Up Dreams Competition**

COLOURING FUN!

Carefully colour the Dressing-Up Dreams picture on the next page and then send it in to us.

Or you can draw your very own fairytale character. You might want to think about what they would wear or if they have special powers.

Each month, we will put the best entries on the website gallery and one lucky winner will receive a magical Dressing-Up Dreams goodie bag!

Send your drawing, your name and your address on a postcard to:
Lily's Dressing-Up Dreams Competition

UK Readers:	**Australian Readers:**	**New Zealand Readers:**
Hodder Children's Books	Hachette Children's Books	Hachette Livre NZ Ltd
338 Euston Road	Level 17/207 Kent Street	PO Box 100 749
London NW1 3BH	Sydney NSW 2000	North Shore City 0745
kidsmarketing@hodder.co.uk	childrens.books@hachette.com.au	childrensbooks@hachette.co.nz